On the First Day of Grade School

On the First Day of Grade School

by Emily Brenner
illustrated by Bruce Whatley

HARPERCOLLINSPUBLISHERS

On the First Day of Grade School

Text copyright © 2004 by Emily Brenner

Illustrations copyright © 2004 by Bruce Whatley

www.harperchildrens.com

Library of Congress Cataloging-in-Publication Data

Brenner, Emily.

On the first day of grade school / by Emily Brenner ; illustrated by Bruce Whatley. — 1st ed.

p.   cm.

Summary: In this cumulative rhyme based on "The Twelve Days of Christmas," a teacher receives an array of animals
from her adoring students.

ISBN 0-06-028013-1 — ISBN 0-06-051041-2 (lib. bdg.)

[1. Animals—Fiction. 2. Teachers—Fiction. 3. Schools—Fiction. 4. Stories in rhyme.] I. Whatley, Bruce, ill. II. Title.

PZ8.3.B7475 On 2004

[E]—dc21   2002014921

                                                                                                      CIP

                                                                                                      AC

Typography by Al Cetta   1 2 3 4 5 6 7 8 9 10   ❖   First Edition

For Anne

—E.B.

For Laura, who's great with kids and animals

—B.W.

On the first day of grade school,
my students gave to me

A python
        that didn't squeeze me.

On the second day of grade school,
my students gave to me

    Two buzzing bees
    And a python
       that didn't squeeze me.

On the third day of grade school,
my students gave to me

Three fat rats
Two buzzing bees
And a python
    that didn't squeeze me.

On the fourth day of grade school,
my students gave to me

    Four burping goats
    Three fat rats
    Two buzzing bees
    And a python
       that didn't squeeze me.

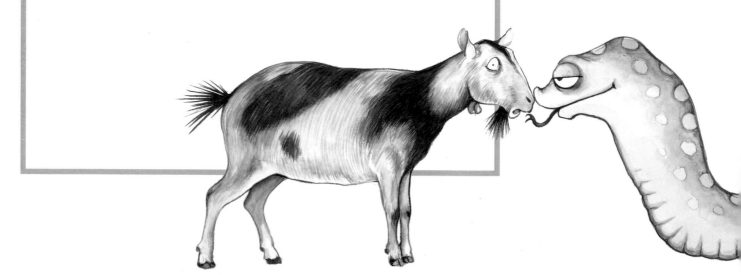

On the fifth day of grade school,
my students gave to me

Five snoring pigs!
Four burping goats
Three fat rats
Two buzzing bees
And a python
that didn't squeeze me.

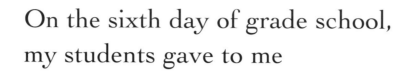

On the sixth day of grade school,
my students gave to me

Six screaming chickens
Five snoring pigs!
Four burping goats
Three fat rats
Two buzzing bees
And a python
that didn't squeeze me.

On the seventh day of grade school,
my students gave to me

    Seven skating monkeys
    Six screaming chickens
    Five snoring pigs!
    Four burping goats
    Three fat rats
    Two buzzing bees
    And a python
       that didn't squeeze me.

On the eighth day of grade school,
my students gave to me

      Eight sick gorillas
      Seven skating monkeys
      Six screaming chickens
      Five snoring pigs!
      Four burping goats
      Three fat rats
      Two buzzing bees
      And a python
         that didn't squeeze me.

On the ninth day of grade school,
my students gave to me

    Nine skunks a-stinkin'
    Eight sick gorillas
    Seven skating monkeys
    Six screaming chickens
    Five snoring pigs!
    Four burping goats
    Three fat rats
    Two buzzing bees
    And a python
       that didn't squeeze me.

On the tenth day of grade school,
my students gave to me

Ten toads on tiptoe
Nine skunks a-stinkin'
Eight sick gorillas
Seven skating monkeys
Six screaming chickens
Five snoring pigs!
Four burping goats
Three fat rats
Two buzzing bees
And a python
   that didn't
      squeeze me.

On the eleventh day of grade school,
my students gave to me

    Eleven prancing ponies
    Ten toads on tiptoe
    Nine skunks a-stinkin'
    Eight sick gorillas
    Seven skating monkeys
    Six screaming chickens
    Five snoring pigs!
    Four burping goats
    Three fat rats
    Two buzzing bees
    And a python
        that didn't squeeze me.

On the twelfth day of grade school,
my students gave to me

Twelve smart zookeepers
Eleven prancing ponies
Ten toads on tiptoe
Nine skunks a-stinkin'
Eight sick gorillas
Seven skating monkeys
Six screaming chickens
Five snoring pigs!
Four burping goats
Three fat rats
Two buzzing bees
And . . .

A python
who'd never squeeze me!

Class of 2